ROCKY MOUNTAIN NATIONAL PARK

Peril on Longs Peak

Adventures with the Parkers

Mike Graf

ILLUSTRATED BY
Marjorie Leggitt

Photo credits:
Licensed by Shutterstock.com: Title page; 1: © Alfie Photography; 4: © John McLaird); 5; 7; 8; 11 (all); 12; 13: © Steshkin Yevgeniy; 14–15; 16–17; 18 (top); 18 (bottom): © Nelson Sirlin; 21; 22; 24; 25: © martellostudio; 28; 30; 33; 36; 40: © Christopher Jackson); 51; 71; 76: © Olga Lipatova; 81: © Christopher Jackson; 87; 89; 94; inside back cover
© Mike Graf: 10 (all); 23; 32; 43; 45; 54; 61; 63; 64; 66; 67; 69; 72; 74; 86
Map courtesy of National Park Service

Cover image: Marjorie Leggitt
Models for twins: Amanda and Ben Frazier

Project editor: David Legere

Library of Congress Cataloging-in-Publication Data is available on file.

ISBN 978-0-7627-7970-3

Printed in the United States of America
10 9 8 7 6 5 4 3 2 1

It was the night before the Parkers left for their trip, and Dad was waiting in the on-deck circle at his softball game. In the last inning of the series against the Storm, Dad's team, the Pilots, were behind 10–9.

The bases were loaded, and Dad's teammate Sean was at bat. Sean swung and lifted the ball to deep left field. It looked like the winning hit, and Sean raced toward first base with his arms triumphantly raised into the air…

The speedy left fielder ran back quickly and caught the ball. All the runners scampered back to their original bases while Sean dejectedly jogged back to the dugout. Now there were two outs, and it was up to Dad to try and bring home a victory.

Dad stepped up to home plate and dug in.

"Come on, Robert!" one of Dad's teammates called out.

The first pitch arched in and plopped onto the mat.

"Striiiike!" the umpire yelled.

The next two pitches were balls. Then Dad fouled one off.

"Two and two!" the umpire called, announcing the count.

Dad stepped out of the box and turned to the dugout. He noticed his whole team was standing and watching.

He took a deep breath and glanced around. His teammates were lined up against the fence in anticipation. Dad also noticed Morgan, James, and Mom sitting in the bleachers.

"You can do it!" Morgan called out.

"Let's go, Dad!" James added.

Dad stepped back up and focused straight ahead.

The pitcher lobbed the ball toward home.

Dad watched the softball approach then swung hard as it crossed the plate. He lined the ball to the left of the shortstop and took off, running toward first.

At the same moment, the shortstop dove and knocked the ball down.

The runners ran full speed toward home, hoping to score the winning runs.

The shortstop pounced on the loose ball and for a brief second grinned confidently, then wound up for his throw to first.

Dad sprinted faster.

"Ahh!" Dad suddenly screamed. He immediately stopped and hopped around before limping the rest of the way to the base. The ball got to first well before Dad.

"Out!" the umpire yelled.

The game was over.

Dad bent over and let out a large sigh. Then his teammates filed somberly onto the field.

Players on both sides met and shook hands. Dad joined them while trying not to grimace as he walked along.

Sean put his arm on Dad's shoulder. "Are you all right?"

"I don't know. Something popped in my ankle."

Several of Dad's teammates came over and consoled him. "It's okay," one said. "We play them again next week. We'll beat 'em then."

"I won't be here," Dad responded. He pointed toward his family in the stands. "We're taking off to Rocky Mountain National Park in the morning."

"I certainly would choose that over softball!" Sean remarked.

Dad said good-bye to his team and hobbled over to his family.

"We'll have to put some ice on it at home," he said. "But I think it's just a sprain. I bet by the time we're hiking in the park I'll be fine."

"I don't know," Mom said worriedly. "It looked like you were really hurting out there."

Then Dad changed the subject. "Are we all packed up?"

"All ready to go," Mom replied.

Morgan, James, Mom, and Dad drove west along Highway 70. They had flown into Denver the day before, stayed in a hotel, and rented a car. Now, with a large line of prominent snowcapped peaks of the Rockies looming ahead, the Parkers got into the spirit of the scenery.

Dad cranked up the CD of John Denver and the family sang along:

And the Colorado Rocky Mountain high
I've seen it rainin' fire in the sky
I know he'd be a poorer man if he never saw an eagle fly
Rocky Mountain high
Colorado

After the song, Morgan sifted through the stations on local radio.

"Another sunny morning," a radio deejay began before Morgan changed the station.

"Wait," Dad called out. "Go back. I want to hear the weather report."

Morgan quickly turned the radio back.

"Typical summer weather for us folks in Colorado," the reporter continued. "After this beautiful morning, those afternoon thunderstorms should pop up again, especially in the mountains. And look for more of the same tomorrow and the day after…"

Morgan turned off the radio. "Well, now we know what to expect."

The Parkers continued driving west. At Highway 40, Dad turned north toward the town of Granby and the southwest entrance to Rocky Mountain National Park. They passed a large lake and resort area with snowcapped peaks looming ahead. Soon, the family entered the park at the Kawuneeche Visitor Center, just beyond Grand Lake.

They drove along a valley framed by high mountains. Although the road was wet from a rain shower the night before, the morning was sunny and bright. Only a few small, puffy clouds clung to the high peaks surrounding the valley.

Soon they approached a parking lot. Dad pulled the car over at the Coyote Valley trailhead. "Let's take a little walk and stretch our legs," he suggested.

"This will also give us a chance to test the altitude and see how our heart rates and breathing respond," Mom added. "We live at sea level, and we're way above that here."

The family walked onto a flat gravel path. They came to a clearing and gazed at the long, wide valley. Across the way a series of barren peaks pierced the western sky.

Dad turned toward James, who had the park map. "What mountains are those?"

James quickly scanned the map and read to his family. "The first one is Mt. Baker. After that there's Mt. Stratus, Mt. Nimbus, Mt. Cumulus, Howard Mountain, and Mt. Cirrus."

CLOUDY WITH A CHANCE OF...

The Never Summer Mountains are named after these cloud types:

Cirrus: Thin, wispy clouds high up in the atmosphere. They are made of ice crystals.

Cumulus: Puffy clouds that look like floating cotton. They are typical in the mountains on a summer day, indicating fair weather, but they can develop into thunderstorms or vertically growing cumulonimbus clouds, which can bring severe weather, including heavy rain or hail.

Nimbus: Dark gray clouds that bring light rain or snow.

Stratus: Low-lying clouds that touch the ground. They often bring drizzle and are sometimes called fog.

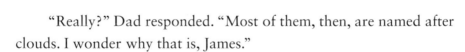

"Really?" Dad responded. "Most of them, then, are named after clouds. I wonder why that is, James."

James looked again. "The map says they're part of the Never Summer Mountain Range. Maybe they're usually covered in clouds."

"Perhaps *that's* why the tops are barren," Mom chimed in. "It's always so cold up there that few plants can grow."

"What's their elevation?" Dad asked.

"They're all over 12,000 feet."

"That's right," Dad remembered. "Rocky Mountain has more than sixty peaks over 12,000 feet in elevation."

Dad gazed at the picturesque mountains. They were mostly cloud-free and basking in sunshine. "They're not exactly living up to their names at the moment," Dad said.

The Parkers continued to stroll along next to a gently meandering stream. Eventually they came to the end of the short path. Mom turned to Dad. "How's your foot?"

Dad thought for a second. "Fine, I guess, along this flat trail." He partially lied, since his ankle had been aching since they left the car. "We'll have to see how it does later."

They turned around and read a few interpretative signs along the trail on the way back. "So this is the start of the Colorado River," Morgan realized while reading one of them.

"Yes," Mom added, "and it goes from here all the way to Baja, California."

"How about we try our first serious Rocky Mountain hike next?" Dad asked.

"Okay by me," James responded.

"Me too," Morgan added.

The family walked back to the car and drove a short distance to another trailhead, just up the road.

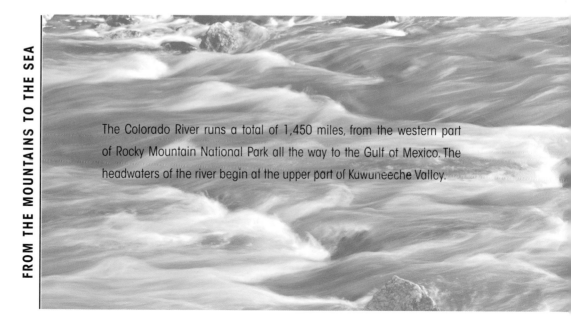

FROM THE MOUNTAINS TO THE SEA

The Colorado River runs a total of 1,450 miles, from the western part of Rocky Mountain National Park all the way to the Gulf of Mexico. The headwaters of the river begin at the upper part of Kawuneeche Valley.

After parking the car at the trailhead, the family got out and packed for their hike to the Little Yellowstone area. Dad also took his Ace bandage. "Just in case," he announced.

The trail was mostly flat, with just a few short climbs. To the west, the Never Summer Mountains poked above the puffy cumulus clouds, still small in the morning sky.

The Parkers traipsed along, passing through verdant grassy areas splashed with wildflowers. The plants and needles on the pines glistened with raindrops from the night before.

Morgan took a picture of a purple-petaled flower with a white center.

Mom came over and looked at the colorful bloom. "I think that's the Colorado columbine," Mom said. "It's Colorado's state flower."

Dad gazed at the meadows. "It seems like everything is in bloom."

"It must be because of the short growing season here," Mom realized. "Nine months of the year it's under snow."

"Because of the elevation!" James exclaimed.

"I guess this is as good a time as any to check on that," said Dad, pulling out a small GPS device from his pack. He pressed some buttons, then waited a minute.

James came over. "What is it?"

Dad pressed some more buttons, then looked at the screen. "About 9,000 feet," he announced. He looked at the mountains across the way. "And we're low compared to the peaks up there."

"I'm sure feeling the altitude down here," Mom said. "I'm a little light-headed."

The Parkers spotted a dark shape far out in the valley. They stared as it began to move, then made out the outline of a large body, its head bent down as it nibbled on meadow grass.

The gangly brown animal stood up and peered at the Parkers.

"It's a female moose!" Mom realized. "You know, they are the largest member of the deer family. We don't have them in California, but they obviously live in the Rockies!"

The family watched the moose and then trekked on.

Soon they approached an open, rocky slope. Several more clusters of columbine were splashed in between the rocks. "I can see why they're Colorado's state flower!" Morgan called out while taking a picture.

"Yeah, the whole area looks like a garden nursery," Mom added.

Dad stopped and stretched his leg out on a rock. He bent forward and cringed while rubbing his foot.

"How's it feeling?" James asked.

Dad put his leg back down and draped his arm around James. "I'll be fine," he replied. "It just gets a little tight when we stop."

The family crossed a footbridge over Crater Creek. From there the area became more forested, with Engelmann spruce and lodgepole pine.

Lulu City was once here.

Birds chirped in the trees. A short time later they approached an old, dilapidated cabin just off the trail. A sign was nearby. Lulu City Site: 1879–1884, population 200, it read.

The Parkers walked around the area. They noticed several spots nearby where the forest had been cleared. "I wonder if another cabin used to be over here?" James mused.

Morgan gazed at the whole area, trying to imagine what it looked like during its heyday. "I remember you told us that there was gold and silver mining and lots of fighting in this town," she said to her parents.

"Ah, the Wild, Wild West," Dad commented. "But they didn't find much to mine, and it cost too much to get what they did. So the whole town was abandoned by 1884."

"And it's still empty now," James said.

After spending a few more minutes there, the family trekked on.

At one point, Mom stopped next to a grove of tall, thin, white-barked trees. "Aspen!" she exclaimed. "A Colorado icon."

Aspens, a Colorado icon.

Mom stopped to take a closer look at the aspen grove. Then she said, "You know, these trees are actually all connected by their root system. And some groves last for thousands of years by spreading their roots out to make new trees."

"And their leaves turn a spectacular gold in the fall," Dad added.

As the day pressed on, James noticed the Never Summer Mountains were more obscured. "What kind of clouds do we have up there now?" he asked Dad.

Dad checked the sky. "Building cumulus clouds. They indicate a potential storm."

The puffy clouds from earlier had merged together. Several leaden gray ones now clustered in the sky. Dad checked his watch. "11:30," he announced. "It looks like the weather report was right: afternoon showers could be arriving shortly."

The family hiked on anyway, staying in the semiprotection of the trees. Soon they crossed a footbridge over a large, boulder-strewn streambed. Then the trail climbed a ridge. The family came to a rocky promontory overlooking a sparsely treed, steeply sloped canyon with colorful rock outcroppings.

"The Little Yellowstone area, I imagine," Dad said.

The Parkers snacked there, just as large drops of rain began plunking down.

After hiking quickly out of the Little Yellowstone area, the family retraced their steps, skirting the side trail to Lulu City. They hiked through scattered showers with rumbles of thunder sounding in the distance.

When the Parkers finally returned to the trailhead, it was late afternoon. The roads were wet, but the rain had stopped, though it appeared to be only an interlude before the next shower.

The family checked the map, noticing a campground nearby. "I think it's best that we stay here at Timber Creek tonight," Mom said.

"Yep, driving over Trail Ridge Road in a possible heavy rainstorm probably isn't a good idea," Dad agreed.

The Parkers drove the short distance to the campground. They quickly found a site, set up their tent, and began to cook dinner.

While the family was gathered around the picnic table, large raindrops began splashing down.

James scanned the gray skies. "Are those cumulonimbus clouds?"

"Yes," Dad started to answer. But the sky did the rest for him, echoing a distant drumroll of thunder. Dad then finished his thought: "They typically bring thunderstorms."

It started raining harder. Mom turned off the stove and dished out the pasta. "I guess we'd better eat quickly!"

With the hoods from their jackets pulled over their heads, Morgan,

James, Mom, and Dad began spooning in the steamy, savory food. But the storm intensified, and the family raced to eat before it got too cold or wet.

As the shower continued, the family took their bowls and stood outside in the rain.

Light flashed across the campground. James counted, "One…two…three…four…five…six…seven…eight…nine…," then thunder rumbled, this time louder. "The lightning's about two miles away," James estimated.

FLASH TO BANG

Lightning is always followed by thunder. To estimate how far away lightning is, people can use the Flash to Bang Method. When there is lightning, count how many seconds until you hear thunder. If it takes five seconds for the thunder to arrive, the lightning is a mile away. If it takes ten seconds, it's two miles distant. If lightning and thunder are nearly simultaneous, be extremely wary; this means lightning can strike nearby at any time! If you are outside in these conditions, stay away from metal, get low to the ground without lying flat on it, get away from tall objects, and spread out from a group, making yourself as small as possible.

Dad looked around while the hood of his jacket dripped fresh rainwater into his pasta. He laughed at his predicament.

Morgan was first to finish her dinner. She quickly began cleaning up. Then James and the rest of the family joined her. They hastily washed dishes,

brushed their teeth, and scrambled to put all their gear away before jumping into the tent.

By then it was really pouring. The rain pounded onto the top of the tent and thunder rumbled intermittently.

The Parkers changed clothes and got into their sleeping bags. It was 8 PM. "What do you want to do now?" Morgan asked.

"Play cards?" James suggested.

Morgan, James, Mom, and Dad scooted closer together. They set up a playing area on a dry towel. Soon Dad was shuffling a deck of cards while the pounding rain continued to serenade them. "I have a feeling we're going to have to get used to this," Dad said.

• • •

The next morning, the Parkers slept in.

It was cool, shady, and wet out when Dad returned from the bathroom. "It's 38 degrees," he reported to his still-snuggled-up family. "But at least the skies are clear."

Eventually sunlight filtered through the trees and began to dry up the area. Finally, after 9 AM the Parkers got up and ate breakfast. They took their time packing, and in the late morning they started their journey up Trail Ridge Road, the highest continuous paved highway in the United States.

As the family began their drive up Trail Ridge Road, Dad noticed the pavement was dried out from the morning sun. "It doesn't even look like it rained here last night," he said.

Dad drove slowly while carefully maneuvering the car around several tight turns. Finally, at Farview Curve, Dad pulled the car into a small parking area. The family got out and gazed at the grassy meadows of Kawuneeche Valley far below.

James checked the sky. "Are those cumulus clouds?" he asked Dad.

"Yep," Dad responded. "If we were in San Luis Obispo, they would most likely mean fair weather. The cool ocean temperature nearby just doesn't allow our air to warm, rise, and destabilize into clouds on a summer afternoon. But here in the Rocky Mountains, those clouds probably portend another round of you know what."

The family piled back into the car and resumed their climb.

Soon they reached Milner Pass. The elevation sign there read 10,758. "Boy, we're high up now," Mom announced.

Dad pulled into another small parking area, at Poudre Lake. Mom pointed out a sign nearby. "We're right on the Continental Divide!"

"So," James thought for a moment, "that means all rivers east of here flow to the Gulf of Mexico, then to the Atlantic Ocean."

"And one foot west, they all flow to the Pacific," Morgan added.

"You both get As in geography," Mom confirmed, smiling.

The Parkers walked along a trail crossing over the divide. A short while later, Mom checked the time. "It's almost noon," she reported. "Should we head back and drive on?"

So they did, stopping to have a picnic lunch along the shore of Lake Irene.

Soon the family was back in the car. The road really climbed now, and the forest quickly thinned out. Trail Ridge Road emerged above the tree line.

Morgan noticed clouds billowing across the sky. "It's like we're right up there with them!" she exclaimed.

"We might as well be, with the way this car is driving," Dad complained. "It's losing its oomph as we gain elevation."

The Parkers approached a large, busy parking lot. Dad pulled into the Alpine Visitor Center area, and the family piled out—and immediately realized how cold it was. They all grabbed jackets and ponchos, and Dad also dug out his thermometer and GPS, packing them into a backpack.

Their eyes were immediately drawn to a line of hikers climbing a steep, wide trail at the end of the lot. At the beginning of the path a warning sign read: DO NOT ASCEND THIS TRAIL WHEN THUNDERSTORMS ARE THREATENING.

In the land of tundra.

Mom glanced up and saw the thick gathering of clouds. "I guess we can try hiking for a little bit," she said warily.

As soon as they started walking, Dad pulled out his GPS. He fumbled with some buttons and a moment later checked the reading. "Just like the sign said, 11,796 feet," he announced.

"I think that's the highest elevation I've ever been at," James said.

Morgan looked up the trail. "Not for long!"

The Parkers climbed the walkway. Their labored breathing kept them moving slowly. Along the path, small signs identified tiny plants and flowers of the tundra's short summer-growing season. "Moss campion," Mom called out at one sign.

Later the Parkers passed by several other labeled flowers of the tundra world. "Alpine forget-me-not. And sky pilots—they're my favorite," Morgan said.

"It's nice they have a distinct walkway to keep us off the fragile, tiny plants," Mom said.

A quarter of a mile up, the trail leveled off. A small bench sat next to the path. Morgan placed her camera on the back of the bench so she could take a picture of her family using the timer. She gazed through the lens. "Hey! Look!"

In the distance a large bull elk pranced across the meadow. The elk paused and looked toward the Parkers, then it continued on, stopping to nibble on some tiny shoots of grass.

Morgan took a photo of the elk, then set the timer to take one of her whole family.

Mom noticed a path continuing beyond the bench and glanced up at the sky. "Shall we go a bit farther?"

The Parkers walked along, moving faster on the flatter section of the path.

Soon they approached a small pile of rocks. Visitors gathered there, signaling that it was the end of the trail.

Dad clambered up the rock pile. He stood on top, held out his GPS, and announced, "12,005 feet!"

James noticed a sign nearby that also identified the elevation. "That's 2.3 miles above sea level," he read.

The sky was dark. Leaden clouds billowed about. A cool, stiff breeze accompanied the clouds. Dad checked his thermometer: "Forty-six degrees," he told them.

"Boy, summers here are colder then our winters!" Mom exclaimed.

A few tiny white balls began to drop out of the clouds. James ran to pick one up and examine it. "It's ice!" he called back to his family. The tiny pieces of hail blew across the ground, then quickly melted.

Dad glanced up at the clouds. "It's coming!" he said.

"Then it's time to head back," Mom said.

The family jogged back to the bench area. Pellets of hail continued to come down sporadically, then let up.

At the top of the wide walkway, the Parkers paused briefly, noticing some visitors still heading up. The family continued down just as another curtain of hail swept over them.

James inspected a hailstone that took longer to melt. "Some of them are marble-sized now," he assessed.

Suddenly the hail started pelting down, ricocheting off the ground. In an instant, everything was getting coated in white. The Parkers shielded their eyes and put their hoods up. Then they scampered down, heading for the safety of the nearby store.

The family ran across the parking lot as hail sprayed down and caromed around like marbles being thrown from the sky. The Parkers finally reached the door and Dad held it open, escorting his family into shelter.

It was a completely different world inside. Visitors strolled around, shopping. Morgan noticed there was even a small café. Then she looked at her shivering brother.

Mom saw James too. "Come on," she suggested. "I think it's time for some hot chocolate."

The family sat down in the little restaurant, next to a window. They stared outside, watching the landscape get coated more heavily in white while a waterfall of icy water cascaded off the roof.

After everyone got hot drinks and some snacks, James took out his journal and wrote:

This is James Parker reporting from the store on Trail Ridge Road.

This road is the highest-elevation paved highway in the United States! Soon we'll be passing the summit at over 12,100 feet. (That is, if this storm ever clears.) Mom and Dad said that will be the highest elevation they've ever been at.

And to think, our house in San Luis Obispo is about 200 feet above sea level. No wonder we all feel dizzy and light-headed!

Right now it is hailing outside. But across the way I can still make out some steep banks of snow. And although they're hard to spot in this weather, there are a few bighorn sheep nearby! I guess they're used to ice pelting them from the sky.

I hope we don't have to get used to it, though.

Keeping our fingers crossed for sunny summer weather.

James Parker

After finishing their hot chocolate, the Parkers looked at souvenirs in the gift shop and eventually wandered over to the visitor center.

Morgan took out her journal and wrote some notes about what she read there.

Dear Diary,

We're high up in Rocky Mountain National Park. This place is very interesting! I walked around the visitor center here, learning about the land of tundra. In fact, there's no other park quite like it. For example:

About one third of this park, including this area, is in this tundra zone. Tundra means "land without trees," and no wonder trees can't survive—winds in the winter can blow over 150 miles an hour up here. And on Trail Ridge Road it's below freezing for eight months of the year! So small plants only have a chance to grow for six to twelve weeks. According to what I just read, the weather in this part of the park is like being in the Arctic!

What else? Ptarmigans—birds that live up here—change their color in the winter from brown to white so they can blend in.

It's all very interesting to me.

Dad came by and tapped Morgan on the shoulder. "Morgan, when you're finished, we should take a look outside."

A moment later, Morgan closed her journal. Dad guided her to a window. The sun had managed to find a break in the clouds, and the wintry scene outside was now bathed in bright light. Already some of the hail was melting away, exposing the tundra grass again.

Dad turned toward Morgan. "I think it's time for us to head on down the highway."

Morgan and Dad walked outside and met James and Mom. The parking lot was wet, but most of the ice was on the tundra, not on the pavement. The family walked to their car and got in. Mom started the engine and turned on the wipers, pushing away a pile of slushy ice.

A moment later the Parkers were slowly heading east along Trail Ridge Road.

Dark clouds drifted overhead with shafts of sunlight spiking down from them. Small piles of hail were still heaped in a few places next to the road. And the wet pavement emitted steam in the sun.

Mountain National Park, ever since they rereleased peregrine falcons back in 1978. I've noted things like that, as well as how many times I've seen the bird and whether it's a 'lifer' or not."

Morgan looked at the ranger. "What's a 'lifer'?"

"A species I've never seen before in my life."

"Good idea, I'm going to remember that!" Morgan exclaimed.

The group trudged on, heading toward a small grove of tall white-barked aspens. Ranger Charles pointed to the trunk of one. "See those holes? Those are what we call bird apart-ments. Last time I was here we saw different types of birds in each hole."

The group stared at the aspen, wondering what kind of dweller would appear.

"Hey, look over here," someone called out.

In a field opposite the trees, three small birds were flitting about in some brush. The group watched them from a distance. "They look like pine siskins," someone said.

Ranger Charles focused his binoculars on the birds. "Yes, two of them are. But I think one is a

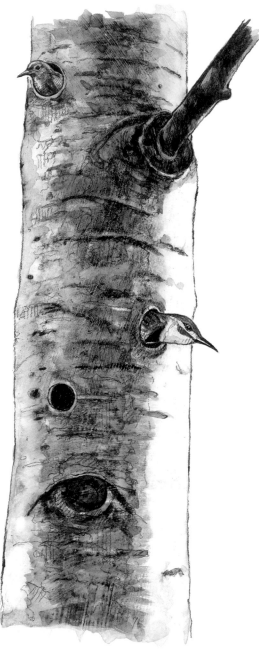

green-tailed towhee," he remarked enthusiastically.

James heard a whistling sound. He quickly scanned the trees. The bird sang again, but James didn't see it. "I wish I could recognize their calls," James said.

Ranger Charles turned toward the Parkers. "I have a book and CD that pairs bird appearances with their songs."

"That might be fun to get," Mom responded, turning toward James and Morgan.

Everyone spread out, continuing to search for more species.

Dad took a second to gaze up at the bright blue morning sky. A few small, puffy clouds were scattered here and there. Like many summer mornings in Rocky Mountain, right now it looked like it would be a beautiful day.

Soon Ranger Charles gathered the group together. They took a quick survey to count the number of species they had spotted: thirteen. "Sometimes, in June or early July, we see a lot more," he informed them. "It's nesting season then, and the birds are a lot more active."

The ranger pointed out some brown, oval-shaped droppings in the grass. "These are from the elk," he said. "They were hunted to extinction here in the 1800s, but then, in the early 1900s, the park introduced a small herd from Yellowstone. That herd grew to the much larger number we have here today."

"We saw some on Trail Ridge Road," James said.

"Yeah, they're all over the park," the ranger explained. "The problem is, the predators that once hunted elk, grizzly bear and wolves, are no longer around. And there are very few mountain lion. So the elk have no natural enemies. I often see them in my yard, in Estes Park."

Then Ranger Charles looked toward a mountain looming far above the rest. "One more thing before we call it a morning," he said. "See Longs Peak up there?"

Training Day #1—Deer Mountain

This is James Parker reporting from the top of Deer Mountain.

It's our first official hike over 10,000 feet in the Rockies. Deer Mountain's elevation is 10,013. There are some trees up here, which Mom says wouldn't be the case if we were in California. Trees stop growing in Rocky Mountain over 11,000 feet.

This is a great hike! And popular too. I can understand why. From a small rocky point we can see all of Moraine Park and Glacier Basin. And we can also see Longs Peak, Thatchtop, and our final training hike for climbing Longs—Flattop, at 12,324 feet.

But maybe there's another reason this trail is so busy today. It's the weather! For once it looks like we won't get drenched with afternoon thunderstorms.

CROSSING THE LINE

Tree line in Rocky Mountain National Park is between 11,400 and 11,500 feet. Tree line exists at this elevation if the mean, or average, daily temperature during the warmest month of the year (July in this case) is 50 degrees. When the highest average temperature is below 50 degrees, trees can't make enough food and sap can't flow, so there is no growth. Also, the season is too short for trees to grow when the highest temperature averages below 50 degrees.

James stopped for a moment and watched Dad as he strutted over to an outcrop of rocks. Dad stepped up on one then looked around, making sure no one else but his family was at the summit.

"Uh-um." Dad cleared his throat as he stood on top of the rock perch. "I'm here to bring you an up-to-the-minute weather report from high in the mountains in Rocky Mountain National Park."

Dad waved his arm across the horizon. "As you can see, it's a beautiful day here on Deer Mountain. And," Dad pointed to the clouds, "right now it's only partly cloudy, with just a few puffy cumulus clouds decorating our skies."

Dad looked at his family, smiled, and continued. "Thunderstorms? Maybe a slight chance later this afternoon. As usual, if you're out in the high country, always be prepared. But, I have to say, today is a great day for a hike in our spectacular Colorado landscape..."

Unbeknownst to Dad, another family of hikers was approaching the summit. They heard Dad and paused to listen.

Morgan, James, and Mom sat together watching Dad's antics as he presented some more. "That's right. Warm, sunny skies today with, believe it or not, temperatures in the seventies, even in the mountains. But remember," Dad emphasized, "every 1,000-foot gain in elevation means a drop in temperature of about three to four degrees, so..."

The other family of hikers strode up, interrupting Dad's report. Dad stopped speaking and stepped off the rock, blushing with embarrassment.

The hikers all clapped.

A person in the group nodded approvingly at Dad. "Thanks for the weather update," he said. "We were wondering if it was going to rain again today."

Dad half smiled, looked away, and said, "Oh, I was just kidding around. Don't take my report seriously."

Dad walked over to his family and sat down. Morgan put her arm around him. "You sounded like one of those weathercasters on TV!"

"You know," Dad reflected, "I always wanted to be a meteorologist."

The family gazed at the views all the way down to Estes Park, far below. Then Mom took out some food for a mountaintop picnic.

Training Day #2—Glacier Gorge

Dear Diary,

It's been a great day in Rocky Mountain National Park! So far this hike has been warm and dry, although I doubt that will last. There are clouds building up and they look like giant cauliflower balloons. In the distance I can see shafts of rain coming down.

But here we are in the sun at Mills Lake. Mom says this spot was made for a picnic. Why? It could be because the waters are sparkling clear. Maybe it's because of the deep mountain bowl the lake is in. Or the rock table we are sitting on. Whatever the reason, it's a popular place. And there are also several people fly-fishing.

What else about the scenery? Well, we are surrounded by mountains over 12,000 feet tall. And above us is Longs Peak—which is over 14,000 feet. Will we all be standing on that throne soon?

Anyway, of all the things to be concerned about in the Rockies (hypothermia, thunderstorms, and altitude), so far today, all is well. I guess, as Mom says, we're getting acclimated. Only James and I now have slight headaches—not bad for being almost 10,000 feet above the elevation at home.

Oops, Mom just nudged me, asking me to pack up. Guess why? The sun just disappeared behind a cloud.

Gotta go!

Morgan

The Parkers made their way back along the same trail they came up. Halfway back to the bus stop, Mom recalled the song from the ranger talk the night before:

Are you hiking?
In the park
Water is essential
Drink, drink, drink.

As Dad sang the second verse, his family echoed the reply:

Are you hiking?
In the park
Don't forget the sunscreen
Put on lots.

James led the third set of words:

Are you hiking?
In the park
Lighting is a danger
Watch for storms.

Eventually the family returned to the trailhead, caught the next bus down, and walked back to camp.

After a few minutes, James again checked the sky conditions. "It's still pouring," he reported. "And there's water everywhere."

"I wonder if we should be thinking about other plans for dinner," Dad pondered.

Mom picked up the park newspaper then glanced at James, who was still looking outside. "Is it showing any signs of letting up?"

"It's hard to tell," James replied.

Morgan slid over to the tent door. She opened it and read Dad's thermometer. "Forty-five degrees," she announced.

"Wow," Dad exclaimed. "It's gotten cold!"

Mom looked at the family. "How about we get out of here?" she suddenly suggested.

The family bundled up and sprinted toward the car. They hopped in and drove through the storm, heading toward the park exit.

On the way out, they passed the Moraine Park Visitor Center. There were a few cars in the parking lot. "Let's check it out," Dad suggested.

It was shortly before 5 PM when the Parkers stepped up to the door. They stood outside for a moment, letting water drip off their clothes.

"Welcome to dry land!" a visitor center employee greeted them once they'd shaken off some of the rain and entered. "You can take a peek inside, but we close in a few minutes."

The family hurried upstairs and quickly glanced at the visitor center displays on elk, mountain geology, and the history of the park.

Then they stepped into a room with large windows, a couple of rocking chairs, and a bench. The family stared out at Moraine Park and the mountains beyond. It was still raining, but the storm seemed to be letting up, at least in this part of the park. Patches of blue sky were now visible between the clouds, and bits of mountain poked through.

Morgan and James sat down. "Now this is the place to watch a storm," James announced.

The visitor center clerk walked in. "That's right," he said, smiling. "We call it our viewing room. Perhaps you can come back tomorrow. We're closing now."

Morgan and James stood up. The family looked out at the park for a moment longer. A solitary peak poked out between the clouds.

Before turning to leave with his family Dad exclaimed, "I think that's Longs. It's way up there!"

By the time they returned to camp after dinner and a walk in the town of Estes Park, it was dark. The storm had stopped and everything was cool and wet. The Parker family went right into their tent and to bed for the night.

The next morning the Parkers again got up early

and trekked over to the Park & Ride area.

"Training hike number three!" Dad announced.

"Or, just another beautiful day in Rocky Mountain National Park," Mom said, looking at the clear blue morning sky.

A short while later the bus arrived. The family piled in and were hauled up the road.

They exited again at the Glacier Gorge trailhead.

Just as they had the day before, the Parkers trekked along, passing Alberta Falls and the junction to Mills Lake. But this time they continued on past The Loch, gaining nearly 1,000 feet elevation along the way.

Eventually the family made it to another junction. "Well," Mom said, "it's either Sky Pond or Andrews Glacier. Which one should we do?"

"I've read great things about both," Dad commented. "But I really want to see a glacier, if that's okay."

The family made their choice and took the trail to Andrews Glacier.

They quickly climbed into an alpine zone, which had fewer trees. Soon they were above the forest completely. The Parkers hiked on through a field of boulders, taking their time to make sure their footing was stable.

James turned to Dad. "How does your ankle feel?"

"Tweaky," Dad replied. "But I'm being extra careful with my steps. Thanks for asking."

Mom paused at one point to let the family rest and regroup. "How's everyone doing?" she inquired.

"I do have a little headache," James admitted.

"Me too," Morgan added. "But I think I'm okay."

"Well, we're over 11,000 feet in elevation," Dad said. "It's understandable that we're having some altitude issues."

James glanced up, trying to pick out the trail beyond where they were. "Hey, look," he pointed.

The family watched two people zigzagging steeply up a slope. "We've got a lot of climbing ahead," Mom realized.

Dad stepped up, leading his family on.

As James followed him, a wave of dizziness engulfed him. He put his arm forward, balancing against a rock. "I don't feel very good," he said to Mom.

Mom watched him for a moment. "Why don't you sit down," she said, guiding James to a flat rock. "I've got a headache too," she admitted.

The Parkers waited there for a few minutes. Then James said, "Okay, let me try again." He stood up, but instantly keeled over and groaned, and immediately sat back down. "You all go up without me! I'll wait here," he cried out, feeling both frustrated and sick.

"You know the only cure for altitude sickness is to go back down," Dad said.

"I don't want you to not finish the trail because of me," James exclaimed.

"I've got an idea," Mom said while glancing at Dad. "Why don't you and Morgan go on? I'll take James back down to the junction and we'll wait for you there."

"Are you sure?" Dad asked.

Mom nodded.

As Dad and Morgan hiked on, up the steepest section of the trail,

James watched them longingly. Then he looked at Mom. "Maybe I'll be okay to go on in a few minutes."

"We'll see," Mom replied. "But it's okay if you aren't."

• • •

A short time later, James stood up and walked a few feet. Then he stopped and held on to a rock. "I don't know," he reported. "I still feel dizzy."

"Come on," Mom said. "This is not a good place to wobble around." Mom put her arm around James and they both began to hike slowly downhill.

Eventually they made it to the junction back in the forest. At this lower elevation, James felt a little better. "I think I could have made it," James said to Mom.

"If you weren't feeling sick from the altitude, I know you could have," Mom replied.

Mom and James sat down, put on an extra layer of clothes, and waited. Eventually they heard Morgan and Dad's voices. They looked up and saw them slogging down the wet, forested trail.

James stood up. "Well, how was it?"

• • •

Later that afternoon they were back in camp. It was sunny and the family took advantage of the weather by hanging out around the campsite. Dad sat in his chair and yawned and stretched. Then he shared some trivia from his book. "It says here that Colorado is one of the top ten states for lightning strikes."

"That's no surprise," Mom responded.

Before dinner, the Parkers decided to take a short walk from the campground up to Sprague Lake. The gravel path around the lake was entirely flat. Morgan, James, Mom, and Dad started strolling along it. "Ahh," Dad breathed. "Finally a trail that's gentle on my foot!"

The calm evening waters of the lake reflected many of the mountains of the Glacier Basin area. James pulled out his map while studying the peaks. The rest of the family gathered around. "There's Thatchtop, Otis, Taylor, Hallett, and Flattop," James pointed out.

James put his map away, and the family continued on their leisurely walk. Nearby, several fly fishermen waded in the water, casting their lines.

Soon they came to an information sign with a bench nearby. Mom, Dad, and Morgan sat down while James went to investigate, pulling out his journal when he returned.

This is James Parker reporting from Rocky Mountain National Park.

Guess what? We hiked to Andrews Glacier today, but I didn't make it. Somewhere between 11,000 and 11,500 feet, altitude sickness kicked in and I had to stop.

Mom stopped too, but I think she did it because of me.

I just read a sign at Sprague Lake. It was about Abner Sprague, who used to run a lodge here. I wonder where it was.

Anyway, one thing he mentioned was that people can always come back next year to see the things they missed.

That makes me wonder about going all the way up Longs Peak. But I wonder if I'm the only one of us wondering that.

Tomorrow we have our last and most difficult training hike, up Flattop Mountain. We'll see how that goes.

It's hard to not finish a hike, though. Dad and Morgan finished one today. Morgan said Andrews Glacier was a large slab of ice dropping into a small lake. And there were even some people climbing on the ice field.

I guess they were acclimated, something I hope to be soon. Dad's reading a book on Colorado's fourteeners. It's about all of the state's mountains over 14,000 feet. Boy, that would be something, climbing all those peaks.

Reporting from Rocky,

James Parker

After hanging out at the lake, the family walked back to camp. While Mom and Dad set up dinner, James and Morgan strolled over to buy firewood.

As they got close, the twins noticed some visitors peering at the field across the way. Morgan and James stepped over. "Look!" Morgan pointed.

Two bull elk were in the meadow, nibbling on grass. One of the elk stopped eating briefly and glanced at the people watching. Then it resumed feeding.

"We'll have to tell Mom and Dad," James said.

"Definitely," Morgan added.

On their final day of training, the Parkers took

one last hike before their attempt to summit Longs Peak on Sunday.

"Over 2,800 feet of climbing today," Dad announced. "And to the highest elevation we've been to so far."

"Today I'm going to make it to the top," James announced enthusiastically.

The family jumped on the now familiar shuttle bus. This time they went all the way to the end of the road.

The first part of their trail skirted Bear Lake. The nature path there was full of people. From that trail, the Parkers took the first of three junctions leading toward Flattop Mountain.

Right away, the path climbed steadily and the views became more expansive with each bend in the trail. At one point, Mom stopped and held a finger to her wrist. "What are you doing?" Morgan asked.

"Checking my pulse," Mom replied. "Let's all do this."

Mom showed everyone how to find their heartbeat. "Okay, count," she said while looking at her watch.

Mom timed them for fifteen seconds. "Stop," she then called out. "Now multiply that number by four."

"128," Morgan said after a moment.

"132," James announced.

Dad's heart rate was around 120. "What's yours?" Morgan asked Mom.

"About what yours was," Mom replied.

The family was stopped in a subalpine zone, which was full of stunted trees. Everyone took a moment to look around. "Hey, there's Sprague Lake down there," Dad realized.

"And Estes Park," Morgan added.

Then Mom noticed thick growth on the base of the trees. "The spruce and fir trees have skirts on them," she said.

"Skirts?" Morgan asked, puzzled.

"Yes, the wind rips off the upper branches in winter blizzards, but the bottom part gets buried in snow and protected from the elements, so that part grows in nice and thick."

Dad then looked up at the sky. "What kind of clouds are those?" he quizzed his family.

"Cumulus!" James responded.

"Yep."

"Cirrus too," Morgan added.

"Right again."

Mom noticed some clouds were whipping across the upper part of Flattop Mountain, partially obscuring the area they were climbing to. "What about those?" she asked.

"They're stratus, low-lying to the ground," Dad replied.

Then Mom had everyone take their pulse again, and they were all now significantly below where they were before. "Good," Mom explained. "We're recovering quickly. That means we're in decent shape and getting used to these high-altitude climbs."

"High-elevation hikers often try to keep their heart rates down by increasing oxygen intake," Mom added. "And it gets harder to do in the thinner air. So what mountaineers do every five to ten breaths or so is fully exhale and inhale like this." Mom forced all the air out of her lungs then breathed in deeply. Morgan, James, and Dad copied her.

"Regular breathing doesn't get rid of all our unused air. This method does. It will help us increase lung capacity."

"And slow down our pulse?" Morgan asked.

"Exactly."

The family continued on its journey. Soon they were completely above tree line, switchbacking up the steep trail.

Mom noticed reflections of the sun shimmering far off to the east. She paused for a moment and stared at the glare. "I think," she mused, "that those are lakes on the Great Plains!"

The family gazed at the distant bodies of water and tried Mom's breathing technique again. "How is everyone?" Mom asked.

"A bit dizzy," Morgan admitted.

"Me too," James said.

"Are you okay to go on?"

Everyone nodded.

James noticed a different trail in the distance. "Hey," he called out, "there are people way down there." James pulled out his map and held it steady in the wind. "It must be this one, to Fern Lake," he pointed out.

Mom leaned over and looked. "Hmm," she pondered.

On a tight switchback, Morgan paused and noticed a lake far below.

James again checked the map. "I bet that's Emerald Lake," he said. "And there's also a trail to it."

"There are a host of options for hiking in this area," Dad realized.

The family kept going, but their pace was now noticeably slower.

Soon they approached a dirty patch of snow and a wooden post. The family again took a few moments to rest, letting their breathing and heart rates slow down. Meanwhile, Dad checked his GPS. "Over 12,000 feet!" he announced. "No wonder we're all short of breath."

Wind whipped about, blowing clouds across the mountain.

James began walking again. "I'm dizzy," he said, "but it seems to get worse when I stop."

The family followed James. Dad glanced at Longs Peak towering in the distance. "I have no idea how Enos Mills climbed that thing over 300 times."

FATHER OF ROCKY MOUNTAIN NATIONAL PARK

Enos Mills moved to Colorado when he was young. While in the Rocky Mountain area, he made forty solo summits of Longs Peak and over 300 total climbs, mostly as a guide. In 1902, Mills bought a house he converted into Longs Peak Inn. From there he regularly led excursions into the mountains. He also measured snow depth, took government surveys, gave lectures, and wrote books. Mills eventually led a campaign to preserve the Rocky Mountain area, and it paid off. The park was created in 1915. He was later nicknamed the Father of Rocky Mountain National Park.

A group of hikers came down the trail, playfully joking and laughing. Morgan noticed how easily they seemed to be walking. She looked at her family after they passed. "They're not even breathing hard!"

The group heard Morgan's comment and stopped. "It's much easier coming down," one of them explained.

"How much farther is it?" James asked.

"You're almost there."

James led the way up the final set of switchbacks. "Come on," he said, urging himself and his family on.

With renewed determination, the Parkers surged toward the summit. A short time later, the trail finally leveled out.

The top of the mountain was a long, flat, and mostly barren plateau. The trail on it was marked by piles of stones, or cairns. Wind whipped about on the peak, and clouds skirted the terrain. The Parkers pulled coats from their packs, bundled up, and carried on, going from one cairn to the next.

Dad caught a glimpse of an ice field hanging down from the mountain to their left. "Hold on a second," he told his family.

He watched more clouds whip by. Dad held his cap down and caught a peek of the slab of ice again. He could see a distinct crack near the top.

The family kept moving forward, following the rock markers. "I'm going to take a quick look at something and be right there," Dad said.

While Morgan, James, and Mom pressed on, clouds enveloped Flattop, creating a gray and foggy scene. They slowly wended their way along the path.

Meanwhile, Dad hopped from rock to rock until he neared a steep drop-off. Ahead of him was tiny Tyndall Glacier hanging precipitously in a deep mountain bowl. Dad stared at the ice sheet, trying to pick out its glacial features.

But the clouds kept obscuring it. And the wind began to make Dad's eyes water. He turned to see if he could glimpse his family, but they were buried somewhere in the fog.

Dad's pulse quickened. He hastily hopped back to the trail. Stepping on a rock, he popped it loose, causing his bad ankle to twist. "Ahh!" Dad called out, wincing. He leaned over and waited for the pain to subside. Then he plowed forward, eventually spotting a trail marker.

Dad sped up. "Honey! James! Morgan!" he called out, but his voice was lost in the clouds and wind.

Dad continued on, picking his way between cairns. Soon, he saw the silhouettes of several ghostlike figures in front of him. One of them was leaning on a sign.

He quickly got close enough to realize it was his family standing at the trail junction along with several other hikers. He hurried until he was within earshot. "I don't think we should separate anymore," Dad announced breathlessly.

"I completely agree," Mom said.

The family stood at the summit watching the wind blow clouds across the mountain plateau.

"Not much of a view right now," Dad managed to say. He quickly checked the elevation. "We're at 12,324 feet," he called out.

"We made it to our highest point yet," Morgan said.

Mom looked at her family, all bundled up and shivering. "Perhaps we should head down now."

As soon as the family dropped off Flattop's summit, the wind calmed down and the clouds dissipated. Beautiful views of mountains, forests, and lakes were visible once again.

The family continued plunging down, eventually making their way back into the forest. There they slowed and shed some of their clothes. While taking off her jacket, Mom looked at Dad. "You know," she suggested, "why don't we all take a day off tomorrow and spend some time in Estes Park? That way we can get some rest and decide if a Longs Peak climb really is the thing to do."

Dad recalled the moment of panic he felt on Flattop when he couldn't see his family. He also thought about his retwisted ankle. "I think that's a great idea," he agreed.

The next day the Parkers took their time in the

morning and waited for the sun to warm and dry their campsite. Finally, they drove into Estes Park, just before noon.

The family's first stop was a Laundromat with showers. "It will feel great to get clean again," Mom said.

"And to wear fresh clothes," Dad added.

After a few hours at the laundry, the family gathered their belongings and left to enjoy the town. As they walked around, Dad ran his hands through his freshly washed hair. "I feel like a new man!" he exclaimed.

Their next stop was a pizza parlor. "It's only three o'clock," Mom said. "I don't know if this will be a late lunch or an early dinner."

"But I'm definitely hungry," James replied, smelling the food.

After eating, the Parkers strolled through the busy village. They saved their excursion into a sporting goods store for last. The family walked inside and started looking around. Mom went over to the clothing section, searching for a tarp and emergency ponchos. Morgan and James browsed the camping and backpacking supplies. Dad noticed books on hiking in Colorado and began skimming through one

After Mom bought the outdoor gear and a birding book that came with a CD, she found Morgan and James. Dad was reading about climbing Longs Peak. He looked up as his family approached. "Oops, sorry, time must have gotten away from me," Dad said. He closed the book. "There's one other thing I need. I'll be just a minute."

"Okay, we'll wait outside," Mom said.

Dad found the backpacking section and inspected the hiking poles.

It was raining again when Mom and the twins stepped outside. They stopped under the store's awning and gazed out at the water-slickened streets. As sheets of rain blew across the road, people rushed to cross the street, covering their heads with jackets or whatever else they had.

Lightning lit up the darkened sky, and thunder boomed loudly. James looked toward the mountains. "I sure wouldn't want to be up on a peak right now," he mumbled.

"I wouldn't want you up there either," Mom replied. "You know, I've been thinking...," Mom began, then stopped.

Dad paid for his book, and he also bought a collapsible walking stick. "Whoa!" Dad exclaimed as he stepped outside. "It's like a whole different day out here."

The Parkers stayed put under the awning, waiting for the storm to let up. But the rain came down even harder, accompanied by intermittent rolls of thunder.

"What did you get?" Morgan asked.

"This," Dad replied, pulling his purchase from its bag. He extended his walking stick then collapsed it. "And it fits in my day pack!"

"Is that for your ankle?" James asked.

"Yep. Just in case."

Mom took a deep breath. She glanced at the twins, and at Dad. "You know," she began again, "I've been thinking."

Dad stopped. He looked at Mom and the kids. Then Dad stared into the rainy street. "I already know what you're going to say."

"Yeah? What's that?"

"You don't want to climb Longs."

Mom paused for a second. "It's not that I don't want to. But what did you expect? I mean, look at the weather we've been having!"

Morgan chimed in. "Dad, I really don't want to go anymore either."

Then Dad looked at James. James shook his head. "I'm not so sure I want to get up and hike right after midnight," James admitted. Then he added softly, "Maybe you shouldn't go either."

Dad sighed. He noticed the sullen looks on his family's faces. "Nobody *has* to go up Longs Peak," he said. "It's something you only do if you really want to." Dad put his arms around Mom. "Can I speak with you over here for a minute?"

Mom and Dad walked over to the next store's awning. Morgan and James watched them. "They're getting upset," Morgan realized.

Lightning flashed in the clouds again. James stared at his parents' animated discussion instead. At one point, Mom shook her head passionately, insistently replying, "*No!*"

"There's electricity in the air now, that's for sure," James commented.

After talking for a few more minutes, Mom and Dad came back over. "Well, we've made a decision," Dad announced.

"And?" James asked.

Mom looked at the twins. "The three of us are going to do that other hike, the Fern Lake loop. We'll go early and try to beat the storms."

Morgan looked at Dad. "And you?"

Dad pondered one last moment. "I'm going to give Longs a try," he replied. "But I promise to be careful. And if there's any sign of bad weather, I'm out of there."

"Okay," they all agreed.

The family hurried back to their car. They drove into the park in the late afternoon. As they turned toward their campground, they passed the visitor center.

Morgan checked the car's clock. "It's past 5 PM," she announced. "It's closed."

"Oh well," Dad said.

"But it was sure nice going into town today," Mom said.

Midnight

Dad's cell phone alarm rang. He snapped up and fumbled with the buttons. It rang again before Dad, half asleep at midnight, was alert enough to figure out how to turn it off.

Dad quietly slipped out of his sleeping bag. He put on warm clothes and his shoes.

Mom rolled over. "Are you sure you want to do this?" she asked.

"I at least want to try," Dad replied. "Ever since I didn't get to the top of Mt. Whitney years ago, climbing a 14,000-foot peak has always been a goal."

Dad slid outside and put his day pack on the picnic table. He glanced around at the ultraquiet Glacier Basin Campground in Rocky Mountain National Park. A light sparkle of frost coated the windshield of the Parkers' car, and a zillion stars twinkled above. *Well, the sky's clear now*, Dad reassured himself.

Dad gathered his gear together in the car. He stepped outside, zipped up his jacket, and checked his watch. "12:25 AM," he whispered. "I'd better get going."

Dad tiptoed back to the tent, unzipped the door, and crawled inside.

Both Morgan and James were awake now. The family looked at Dad, all bundled up. "You look like you're heading to Alaska," Morgan commented.

"It kind of feels like that to me," Dad replied. "It's icy outside."

Dad reviewed his plans with Mom, then he hugged everyone good-bye.

"Good luck!" James called out.

"Be safe," Mom added.

"You three too," Dad said.

Dad slid out of the tent, walked briskly to the car, and started it. He left the car in park and stepped outside to scrape the frost off the windshield, then quickly hopped back in and cranked up the heat. He ran the wipers until the window was clear.

Soon he was driving out of the Glacier Basin area and traveling on a highway toward the Longs Peak trailhead. A sliver of the moon shone in the night sky.

• • •

After driving several miles along a stretch of isolated mountainous road, Dad checked the clock: 1:10 AM. *I should be there any minute now*, he told himself.

The sky was still clear, and he could see city lights glowing in the east.

Dad peered ahead at an approaching sign. As he got closer, he realized it was his stop.

Several groups of people were outside their cars gathering supplies in the large, half-filled parking lot. Dad parked the car and pulled out his coat and his thermometer, placing them on the roof. He slipped on his headlamp and began packing, stuffing extra clothes, an Ace bandage, and the collapsible walking stick into his pack.

He then began to do a series of stretches to help loosen up his still-injured foot. Afterward, Dad checked the thermometer: 33 degrees.

The buzz of activity in the parking lot continued. Several other groups of climbers pulled into the lot, while one large party stretched out their legs and backs, preparing for the climb. Finally, many of the climbers headed for the trail.

After watching a few parties head out, Dad stopped stretching. He locked up the car and found the trailhead registry, where he wrote his name, his destination, and his departure time. It was 1:30 AM when he began the trek toward the summit.

As Dad huffed along the path, steam poured out of his mouth with each breath. He thought of the peak ahead. The obstacles he had read so much about sifted through his mind: the Boulderfield, the Keyhole, the Narrows, and the Trough were somewhere up there, waiting.

1:45 AM

Dad plowed on, continuing his nighttime climb. His headlamp illuminated a small circle of light around him. Just out of the range of the light, a deep, dark, ghostlike forest lined both sides of the trail.

According to Dad's watch, it was 1:45 AM. Suddenly, out of the dark, a sign appeared just past the half-mile marker: Eugenia Mine Trail junction. *I wonder what's out there?* Dad thought. Then he estimated the miles left to the summit. "Only seven to go," he joked out loud.

Dad pressed on. His foot, although stiff and sore from over a week of hiking on the injury, was functioning well enough at the moment. And the high-altitude training seemed to have paid off: Dad's lungs felt strong. *I must be over 10,000 feet now*, he estimated.

Dad's midnight trek began to take on a rhythmic feel. One step followed the other, and then another. Even Dad's breathing, although louder and faster than normal, kept a steady beat.

Dad turned a corner and heard voices ahead. Then he saw two lights. But the lights weren't moving. Soon Dad caught up to a couple of people wearing headlamps. He hiked by, noticing they were shedding a layer of their clothes. *They must be sweating*, Dad realized. He wondered if he, too, should take off his jacket.

The thought passed and Dad surged on. Above, he saw hundreds of stars peeking through breaks in the forest. To the east, an occasional glimpse of city lights from Boulder, Longmont, and Denver reminded Dad that civilization wasn't all that far away.

In Dad's half-awake, dreamlike state, his mind began to drift. He thought of his book in the tent, *Colorado's Fourteeners*, and all the other 14,000-foot peaks in the state. *And I'm climbing one of them*, Dad thought, taking pride in himself and cherishing the potential accomplishment. *Maybe I can get an* I Climbed Longs Peak *T-shirt in Estes Park afterward*.

A sign near another junction read Goblins Forest Backcountry Campsite. Dad paused there for a moment, focusing in on the ghostlike trees that lined the trail before they disappeared into the darkness farther below. *It does seem that goblins could live out here*, he thought. Then Dad checked the small thermometer dangling from his jacket. It registered 36 degrees. *I wonder if I'm warming it from my exertion*, Dad considered. *It feels a lot colder than that*. The night, elevation, and frosty air definitely had a bite to it.

The long, lonely hike in the dark continued. *Shouldn't I be in bed now?* Dad thought, laughing as he yawned. *Is this really what I chose to do on my vacation?* He smiled and pressed on.

Then, out of the dark, another sign suddenly appeared.

Warning: LIGHTNING HAZARD
When electrical storms approach, turn back if possible.
Avoid high points, horses, ridges, and campfires.
Take shelter in low pockets away from tall trees.

Dad read the ominous warning then looked at the clear skies. He walked on, suddenly realizing that the forest was disappearing.

Now, from what Dad could discern, only small, stunted trees grew along the trail. A full display of stars was visible above.

I'm in the krummholz zone, Dad realized, *approaching tree line.*

ARCTIC TREES

Krummholz trees grow near timberline in the Rocky Mountains. Repeated exposure to blasting winds and freezing temperatures causes the vegetation to be stunted and deformed. Oftentimes these trees grow more densely near the ground, where the branches are more protected from the elements.

A tiny shooting star whisked across the sky, then quickly faded. *A meteorite,* Dad said to himself, *entering our atmosphere and burning up.*

Far ahead Dad noticed another headlamp bobbing up and down. He focused his eyes on the beacon, but it kept moving. Two other lights were beyond the first one. The signals illuminated the path up the mountain.

Dad recalled Morgan and James's class performance of the poem "Paul Revere's Ride." "One if by land and two if by sea," Dad chanted.

Dad let his mind run with the thought, and he reworded the poem:

Listen, my family, and you shall hear
Of the midnight walk of Robert Parker here
On July 27, on a night very late,
I climbed to the stars, far up into their gates

Dad paused and snickered to himself, *I'm not a very good poet.* But, with nothing else to keep him occupied, he tried a few more lines.

You know the rest, about my hike I once said
How Robert Parker never stopped nor fled
Though altitude and elements gave him a fight
He made it up the mountain just before the end of night
Then at dawn crossed the Boulderfield, only to emerge
At the Keyhole figure, causing his energy to surge
Dad pressed on to the summit, with backpack in hand,
Pushing toward the top while in full command
And what a beautiful site he beheld far below...

"Hmmm." Dad smiled to himself as he spoke aloud. "Not bad, eh?"

Dad got ready to spin his next stanza when another sign interrupted his thoughts: Battle Mountain Camp.

Dad pulled out a small map and shone his headlamp on it. "I must be near 11,000 feet now," he said. "That means only five miles to go! But still over 3,000 feet of elevation gain."

Dad now noticed a line of lights ahead of him and several bobbing behind. He checked his watch: 3:15 AM.

3:30 AM

As Dad's magic hike under the stars continued, he slowed briefly to pull out his GPS. Dad pressed some buttons and held it out. "11,500 feet," he announced to himself.

Dad's pace relaxed. The air was cooler at this altitude too. His dangling jacket thermometer registered 32 degrees.

Ahead, looming in the night sky, Dad could barely make out the dark silhouette of a massive mountain. *There's a monster up there*, he thought. He kept climbing, following the line of lights ahead and being trailed by several below.

Eventually another phantom sign appeared out of the dark, this one for the Chasm Lake junction. *Okay, 11,600 feet now*, he realized after glancing at his small map. *Only four miles to the summit.*

He slogged on, pushing harder to keep a steady pace. His breathing became labored as he trudged up a set of rock stairs.

Occasional meteorites whisked across the sky. *You know what I wish!* Dad exclaimed to himself, keeping his eyes on the horizon.

Later, Dad approached Granite Pass junction. He looked at the information on his map. *Now I'm past 12,000 feet. This barren, treeless altitude at Rocky is new terrain for me!* The trail began to switchback steeply up. Dad passed by a few tiny trickles of water. He wondered if he'd recognize the location in daylight, in case he needed to filter up on the return trip.

Dad surged on, but then suddenly stopped and shone his light all around. He quickly scanned the area, searching for the worn pathway. *Am I even on the trail?* he wondered, his heart beginning to pound. *When did I lose it and where?*

Dad backtracked several steps. To his relief, he soon found the path and continued upward.

I better watch my steps more carefully, Dad coached himself, *and keep my GPS at the ready.* Then he glanced east. The lights of the cities appeared slightly dimmer. A faint glow was beginning to appear above the horizon. It was 4:50 AM.

4:50 AM

The ever-so-slight hint of daylight on the mountain slowly increased. Dad still used his headlamp to watch his footing, but the darkened world around him was now coming into view.

As Dad continued, the shoulder of massive Longs Peak began appearing. Just below the face of the mountain, Dad could barely make out a tiny snowfield. *That mountain really* is *a monster*, Dad realized.

Up ahead a shelter emerged out of the darkness. Dad also noticed people moving around. Like him, they were still using their headlamps. But, for the first time on the hike, Dad could see people attached to the lights.

Dad pressed on. Straight ahead were two small structures propped up on rocks. "The privies," Dad realized. He decided to use them and got in line. As he waited, he glanced at his thermometer: 31 degrees. Then he checked the elevation note on his little map: 12,760 feet!

After a person exited, Dad climbed some stairs and stepped inside.

Within a few minutes, he had returned to the trail. By now dawn was fully breaking. Dad turned off his headlamp and resumed his ascent.

He felt a renewed sense of energy knowing he was now at the 5.9-mile mark. He had less than two miles to go.

Dad scrambled to the top of a large boulder. He stood and gazed out at the emerging horizon.

The Boulderfield, Dad recalled. *That must be where I am now.*

The sky was partly cloudy. *Mostly altocumulus*, Dad realized. The higher clouds meant no thunderstorms, *at least for the time being*, he concluded.

Dad scanned the area, trying to gauge where the trail was. He could see people above him scrambling up the main part of the Boulderfield. At the top of the rocks a zigzag-shaped slot cut into the mountainside. The notch now held a tiny human-shaped silhouette. The person waved to someone near Dad.

The Keyhole, Dad realized. He clambered on as quickly as he could, then immediately slowed down. Suddenly Dad felt light-headed. *Either from lack of sleep or the elevation*, he thought. *Or both.*

It was now 5:40 AM.

• • •

James popped out of the tent at Glacier Basin Campground. The area was again coated with a light frost. James walked around and found a clear view of Longs Peak. From that vantage point he gazed up at the massive mountain.

The jagged rock profile of a beaver appearing to climb toward the summit was just where it was yesterday—still separated from the peak.

The world isn't going to end yet, James concluded, remembering the legend from the bird walk.

James checked the sky. It was mostly clear below, but a few high clouds enshrouded the mountain. *Good climbing weather for Dad*, James thought. *And good hiking weather for us.*

James strolled back to the tent and reported the conditions to Mom and Morgan. He slid inside and crawled back into his sleeping bag, waiting for the morning sun to thaw the frost.

5:50 AM

Dad scrambled slowly up to the top of another large boulder. He paused there, trying to calm his breathing.

Suddenly the sun lit up the Keyhole formation on the mountain. Dad watched the light creep down toward him. Soon the whole panorama was bathed in bright morning light. It was now a completely new day.

Dad climbed on, scrambling from one boulder to the next. He paused again while putting his head down and leaning over. Dad shut his eyes for a moment and then opened them as two people scurried past. He watched the energetic climbers. *They're half my age*, he realized.

Dad looked around, noticing that the nighttime lights had been completely replaced with faces. There were climbers all over the trail, some below him, and others well past. A few people were even standing in the Keyhole, watching the sunrise.

Dad glanced briefly at Longs Peak, still towering above to his left.

The day warmed quickly, and Dad took a quick glance at his thermometer—40 degrees. *The sun's really radiating off these rocks and warming the air*, he observed.

The climb up the Boulderfield steepened. Dad followed the makeshift path of the people ahead of him. He looked up. *I'm within a hundred feet of the Keyhole*, he encouraged himself.

But those hundred feet took a while. He climbed some more, paused, caught his breath, and scrambled up farther.

Soon Dad approached a small stone shelter just below the Keyhole. He surged on, finally stepping beyond the Boulderfield and into the prominent slot in the mountain.

Dad stood in the Keyhole, admiring the views and his accomplishment. *It's a rock-strewn world up here*, he thought to himself. Lakes and snowfields were scattered among the rocks well below his perch, and beneath that was the forest.

He took a moment to check his GPS: 13,160 feet.

"Wow," Dad gasped. Then he found a rock to sit on and took out a peanut butter sandwich, forcing himself to stop, rest, and eat. It was now 7 AM.

Feeling weak and light-headed, Dad sat a little longer in the Keyhole and slowly managed to swallow part of his sandwich. The sun continued to warm the area. He shed a windbreaker and gulped down some water.

The sky was partly cloudy, but the clouds didn't appear threatening. *They're not really becoming vertical yet*, Dad observed.

People kept scurrying by and saying hi to Dad as they passed. Finally, a couple of young climbers stopped long enough to chat. "How's it going?" the woman greeted him.

"I'm okay," Dad replied. "Just trying to slow down and get some food and rest. I figure a mile or so to the summit can't take that long."

The woman looked at Dad. "Is the altitude getting to you?"

"It must be," he admitted. He found his pulse on his neck and checked it. "But my heart seems to be calming down a bit now."

"Yeah, the last time we climbed Longs, it was here at the Keyhole that the elevation started to take its toll on us," the woman explained. "I started getting dizzy and light-headed from about this point on."

"You've been up here before?" Dad asked. "How long does it take from here?"

"At least two hours with all the rock scrambling and the elevation. It's really slow-going."

"And another couple of hours to get back down to here," the man added. "You really have to watch your step."

The two climbers said good-bye and pressed on.

Meanwhile, Dad added up the estimated times in his head. *So, if all goes well, I won't even be back to this spot until nearly noon*, he realized.

He immediately packed his food and water and stood up.

The world around Dad instantly went into vertigo. He felt as if a carousel of boulders was whirling around him.

Dad wobbled, then tried to steady himself. It felt as if all the blood in his body was being pumped through his head. He started to topple and leaned forward, somehow managing to get his arm out and stop himself from collapsing onto the rocks.

Dad slowly lowered himself back to a seated position. He sat on a rock and tilted his head down until it was between his knees.

Dad stayed in that exact position and waited. Meanwhile, several more climbers hiked past.

7:40 AM

After a few more minutes, Dad slowly lifted his head, hoping the dizziness had subsided. He sat up and watched another group of climbers scuttle by.

Dad stood up and steadied himself against a rock. *So far, so good*, he thought, trying to reassure himself.

Dad plodded along for several steps, making certain as he went that his footing was secure. Soon he made it past the Keyhole and onto the next section of trail. From there, a series of reddish yellow circles painted on the rocks stretched out into the distance.

Dad traversed carefully toward the first circle. Slowly he gained some confidence. A couple of climbers came up behind him. He sensed their presence and paused, letting the faster-paced hikers go by. Quickly they came to a couple of boulders with metal rods sticking out of them. Each grabbed onto the bars and hoisted himself over the obstacle.

Dad maneuvered to the same place. He lifted himself into the slot between the boulders and lowered himself slowly down the other side.

Dad gazed ahead. The colored markers continued across steep, angled rock precipices. Below the makeshift pathway, the mountainside dropped dramatically to the lakes and forest far below. Dad gazed at the whole area, realizing that if he fell, it would be a long tumble over solid stone. He recalled reading about injuries people sustained while climbing Longs Peak. The Trough and the Keyhole were accident-prone locations.

Dad looked ahead. *That must be the Trough coming up*, he thought.

Dad remembered reading that hypothermia, lightning, falls, and disorientation were some of the issues people had faced on Longs Peak. He shook his head and tried to block out the negativity. Dad then noticed climbers hauling themselves farther up the steep mountain. He gingerly shuffled forward, trying to wedge his feet into a small notch in the rock.

But Dad's tentative footing gave out. He slipped onto his knees while managing to grab the rock and hang on.

A solo climber scrambled over to Dad. He put his hand out and helped hoist him back to his feet. "Are you okay?" the mountaineer asked.

"Yeah, I think so. Just being too timid with my steps," Dad replied.

The man waited a moment. "You can go on," Dad said. "Don't stay here for me. I'm not sure what I'm going to do."

Feeling light-headed again, and with his pulse racing, Dad returned to the boulder with the metal rods. He crawled back over and retreated to the Keyhole before sitting down again.

There Dad tried to relax his breathing, and after a while he checked the sky. Clouds were just starting to build up. "That's no surprise," Dad said out loud. Then he checked his watch: 9:55 AM. *Wow*, he realized. *I better think this over.*

A while later, Dad again stood to head for the summit. "I'm just going to go for it," he tried convincing himself. Dad followed the markers back to the spot with the metal rods and slowly pulled himself up.

Two people were coming back the other way. It was the couple who had spoken to Dad at sunrise. Dad recognized them. "Did you make it to the top?" he asked.

"Not quite," the woman answered. "Once you see clouds like these," she pointed to the sky, "chances are likely there will be thunderstorms by noon, or possibly sooner. And being anywhere up here above tree line is not the place to be during a storm," she finished.

"Got it," Dad said. He let the two people scramble past, took one more look toward the summit, and turned around to begin the trek back.

8:15 AM

After sleeping in a bit longer, Morgan, James, and Mom got up to start their hike. They walked from the campsite at Glacier Basin to the Park & Ride bus area.

As they approached the large parking lot, Mom looked up at the sky. "Mostly clear now," she reported.

A few minutes later, a bus arrived. Mom and the twins stepped onto the crowded shuttle and were hauled four miles up, to the Bear Lake area.

The Parkers hopped off the bus at the end of the road. They filled up their water bottles at the drinking fountain and immediately hit the trail at Bear Lake. Many other visitors were also strolling along the picturesque nature path. A short distance later, another path appeared.

"Here's our trail!" James exclaimed.

They took the side path and started along the Fern Lake Trail.

Wearing day packs instead of full-on backpacks, and somewhat acclimated to the elevation, the three Parkers cruised briskly along, soon passing through a grove of aspen thriving in a boulder-strewn area.

"The Rockies are so beautiful," Mom commented while looking at the white-barked trees.

"Look, you can see how the aspen are all growing in one area," Morgan added, "because of their roots."

As the trail gently climbed, Morgan, James, and Mom hiked over remnant patches of snow and past wildflower-filled meadows.

Eventually the trail entered an area of fewer trees. "I think that's Flattop Mountain up there to the left," James pointed out.

Boulderfield Backcountry Campsite, Longs Peak Trail.

• • •

It was approaching 11 AM as Dad worked his way down from the Boulderfield. He continued watching the clouds build up in the sky. Dad also kept glancing at Longs Peak, looming to his right. "One day," he announced to the mountain. "One day!"

Still feeling light-headed and weak, Dad slowly scrambled down a series of large boulders. He stood on the top of one and paused. Far below, Dad noticed the couple who had passed him earlier. He also now saw, for the first time, several stone circles—backcountry campsites he'd missed in the darkness on his way up.

Dad lunged forward to the next boulder. His foot landed awkwardly and twisted to the side. Then the rock wobbled. Dad teetered back and forth before putting out his hands to brace himself for a short fall.

Just then, Dad's foot slipped farther, wedging between two rocks. He felt his ankle tense. "Ahh!" he cried out, wincing in pain.

He keeled over and closed his eyes, holding in a scream. Then Dad slowly sat down and pulled his foot out before gingerly working his shoe off. He grabbed the Ace bandage out of his pack and carefully wrapped his reinjured foot.

Once finished, Dad stood up and tested his foot by carefully putting his full weight on it. His ankle felt sore, but it stayed supported. Dad quickly laced up his hiking boot, then crept down the mountain, even more slowly than before.

Several steps later, Dad's ankle again twinged in pain, but the support wrap stopped it from flipping over.

Dad hiked down carefully. *Going uphill is easier*, he concluded, *as far as my foot is concerned.*

As Dad continued, he suddenly remembered his collapsible walking stick. He paused and wondered if it would help him maneuver around these large rocks. Then Dad checked the sky again. A storm seemed imminent. *A metal stick could soon become a lightning rod*, Dad realized, deciding to leave it in the pack.

Soon the boulders Dad traversed became smaller. He walked past the first of several stone circles. Each enclosed a large enough space for a tent, the rocks piled into walls a few feet high.

All of a sudden, a few white balls of ice began plunking down. Hail. Dad glanced up to see its source: a big dark cloud overhead. "Oh, no," Dad mumbled. Then he scanned the direction of the trail down the mountain. *I have a long way to go before I drop below tree line*, he realized.

• • •

At the trail's summit, the three Parkers took a small side path to a rocky outcrop. They sat down and gazed at the unobstructed views of massive peaks, snowfields, and waterfalls, with Odessa Lake far below.

Mom pulled off her day pack, unpacked some energy bars and fruit, and they picnicked with the high mountain scenery sprawled out in front of them.

A dark cloud obscuring the sun put an abrupt end to their leisurely lunch. "We should head down into the forest and get away from this open area," Mom warned, concerned about lightning.

Morgan, James, and Mom quickly packed up, hurried back to the main trail, and began their descent toward Odessa and Fern lakes.

• • •

Dad moved faster on flatter ground, but he was favoring his injured foot. Meanwhile, the hail intensified, bouncing with force against the trail and rocks.

Suddenly Dad heard a distinct humming sound. His hair rose from his scalp, standing on end. Dad took a second to gauge his surroundings. Then he dove into the nearest backcountry campsite and covered his head.

• • •

Morgan, James, and Mom hiked briskly downhill. They passed a small boulder field and quickly entered the forest surrounding Odessa Lake. Mom and the twins walked past the lake as scattered drops of rain plopped onto the surface. Thunder rumbled in the distance. Mom checked the sky and saw more dark clouds rolling in.

"Where do you think Dad is now?" James asked, worried.

Mom glanced at her watch. "It's just before noon. Knowing how careful Dad is and how much he checks the weather, I'm sure he's far below the peak by now."

The rain began to intensify. Mom hastily pulled out ponchos. They each put one on and continued hiking. Soon they were hurrying along in a steady rainstorm pierced by regular claps of thunder. The trail was becoming soaked.

A short time later, Morgan, James, and Mom arrived at Fern Lake. A side trail led to backcountry campsites and a ranger cabin.

Mom took the twins in that direction. The wooden ranger cabin was perched above the northern end of the lake. The three Parkers hustled onto the deck of the cabin.

Lightning flashed outside followed by instant, deafening thunder. Rain mixed with hail started pounding down.

Mom looked out at the storm while she, James, and Morgan scrunched up against the cabin wall. "We might as well pull up a seat," she said. "It looks like we're going to be here a while."

They sat on the floor of the deck and watched the rain drench the wilderness.

11:35 AM

While hail pounded down all around him, Dad closed his eyes and remained pressed up against the rock wall. He could see lightning flash through his eyelids, followed by booming rounds of thunder.

After a while, Dad peeked out to check the conditions. The precipitation was now a rain and hail mixture. The ice was starting to accumulate.

Dad realized he wasn't going to be able to stay in this spot for long. He recalled that tree line was at least several miles below. *This is not good!* he thought.

Dad hurriedly pulled a poncho out of his pack. He slipped it on and then moved his injured foot around. It felt tight and sore when he flexed it, but also somewhat stable. *It's only going to get worse the longer I sit here*, Dad realized.

Finally the onslaught of precipitation eased a bit and the thunder became softer and less frequent.

Dad stood halfway up. The trail was soaked, but at least he could make it out by hiking around the slushy puddles. Dad glanced at the sky directly above him. Dark gray clouds hovered overhead, and they appeared to be moving briskly along. He wondered if the worst of the storm was coming or going.

The storm let up a bit more. Now only scattered pieces of hail came down, bouncing off the rocks.

• • •

Morgan, James, and Mom remained on the deck of the cabin, watching the storm. Lightning continued to flash intermittently, and thunder rolled across the mountains. The three Parkers stayed bundled up while nibbling on snacks.

"I wonder how Dad is doing," Morgan mused.

Mom glanced at her watch. "Maybe he's taking a break, like we are. It's around lunchtime. He should be down from the summit."

For a while, Morgan, James, and Mom stopped talking about Dad. But they still worried about him. They had seen storms bombarding the prominent peak all week. The family sat and stared, hoping for the weather to change.

• • •

For a brief moment, Dad felt safer and thought the worst had passed. He stood all the way up and inspected the sky. Then he glanced toward Longs Peak, but it was totally obscured. Finally he looked at the Keyhole.

Three tiny figures were standing in the formation, silhouetted by gray clouds.

Dad felt something funny in the air again. He instinctively began to cringe as a long bolt of lightning lit up the sky and illuminated the Keyhole.

Dad immediately ducked back down into a fetal position. Thunder shook the whole region. It sounded like a gigantic monster tossing boulders.

In the midst of the turmoil, Dad thought he heard someone scream. He peeked out, glancing toward the Keyhole, but this time he didn't see anyone.

Then Dad studied the clouds. The darkest ones appeared to be moving away from his location.

Dad stood up again, looking toward the Keyhole. He cupped his hands and shouted, "Is everyone all right up there?"

He stood still and listened, but there was no answer.

"Is everyone okay?" he called out again.

The only sounds he heard were the wind and rain.

Dad thought quickly: *With my ankle, it might take an hour to get back up there. And then what good would I do? I'd only be putting myself in harm's way too. The best thing to do is to head out and tell rangers what I heard as soon as I can.*

Dad checked the Keyhole again.

"Are you okay?" he shouted one last time.

"Okay…okay…okay…" the mountain echoed back.

Dad remembered how bad he felt at the Keyhole earlier. *I probably couldn't even get there now*, he justified to himself.

The weather confirmed for Dad that he was making the right decision. Small balls of hail began plunking down again. He stopped thinking and took off down the trail.

• • •

Eventually a backcountry ranger strode up to the cabin. "Hi, folks!" she greeted the Parkers.

"Hi," they replied. "We're just trying to stay out of the storm," Mom explained. "Is that okay?"

"Of course," the ranger replied. She stood next to the Parkers. "By the way, my name's Dana."

James introduced his family, and then added, "My dad's climbing Longs Peak."

Dana flinched. "Really?"

Mom picked up on Dana's tension. "Why? What's up?"

Dana paused for a second. Then she unclipped her hand radio and glanced at the Parkers. "Just a moment. I want to check on something," she said and stepped into the cabin.

Morgan, James, and Mom stood up and waited. The storm seemed to have eased, and now only a light mist fell. James peeked up and noticed patches of blue between the clouds. "It's clearing!" he announced.

Meanwhile, Mom tried to listen to Dana's conversation on the hand radio inside the cabin. She could hear a muffled, crackly voice and some of Dana's brief replies.

Finally Mom heard Dana say, "Okay, I understand. I'll check in again in a little while." Dana stepped back outside. She looked at Mom and gently probed her with a few questions. "You said your husband is climbing Longs Peak today? Do you know when he left?"

Mom, Morgan, and James now all looked worried. "About 1:00 AM," Mom replied. "Can you tell me what's going on?"

Dana hesitated and took a deep breath. "I don't want to overly concern you, but…"

The Parkers braced themselves for impending doom.

Then Dana continued. "There's a rescue crew heading toward the mountain right now. Details just came in, but there may have been a person or party hit by lightning somewhere up near the Keyhole." Dana paused again then looked directly at Mom. "Was he traveling alone?"

"Yes," Mom answered, trembling with fear.

Dana let out a sigh. "My sources tell me, although again we don't have all the details, that there was a party of three involved. But that doesn't mean a solo hiker didn't join up with a group. Over a hundred people signed the register for a climb to the summit today, and I have no idea who might have been involved in what happened up there.

Since your husband left quite early, chances are he was far below the Keyhole when the storm let loose."

"When was that?"

"Just a little while ago, about the same time as here."

Mom estimated Dad's climb, figuring and hoping he would have been well below the Keyhole by then.

A shaft of sunlight penetrated the forest. It instantly warmed the air, and steam rose off the wet ground. The Parkers quickly packed up.

"Do you know the weather forecast for the rest of the afternoon?" Mom asked Dana.

"More thundershowers," she replied. "But you'll be hiking downhill from here and deeper into the forest. It might be best to head out now, while you can. You've got about four miles to go until you reach the trailhead bus stop."

Morgan, James, and Mom hastily started walking. Dana called out to them as they left: "You can get updated information about the rescue from a ranger at the visitor center or campground. Please take cover if it starts getting stormy again."

The Parkers scurried back to the main trail, turned left, and began hiking out.

1:00 PM

The trail continued to descend. The lower Morgan, James, and Mom went, the denser the forest became. So far, the weather in that part of the park was an improvement over their experience higher up.

The three Parkers tromped by Marguerite Falls and plunging Fern Falls. Eventually they made it to the junction at The Pool. Several other hikers were gathered there, also dressed in jackets.

"I think we can slow down a little bit now," Mom commented. "Let's watch our footing on the wet rocks."

Morgan, James, and Mom relaxed their pace and headed toward the shuttle stop at the Fern Lake trailhead.

When they finally made it to the end of the trail, the rain had completely stopped. The three of them joined a group of others at the bus stop.

Mom checked her watch. "It's nearly 3 PM," she told Morgan and James. "Assuming everything's all right, I don't think Dad'll be that far behind us returning to camp."

James pulled out his map. "The visitor center's on the way," he realized.

"Let's stop there and at least get some information about what's happening on Longs," Mom suggested. "It'll be nice to put our minds at ease."

It started raining again just as the bus pulled up. Morgan, James, and Mom hopped on and rode until they got to the visitor center stop.

They walked inside quickly and noticed two rangers engaged in an urgent conversation. The Parkers stopped and listened for a second.

• • •

After a long trek down, Dad finally made it back into the land of trees. The sky continued to spit out short bursts of rain and hail, but by now, Dad felt better, safer. Even though he was cold and wet, he kept on moving.

Somewhere in the forest, a group of rangers stormed past Dad, rushing up the mountain. "Hey," Dad called out to them. The rangers stopped, and Dad quickly told them about what he saw and where.

"Someone called in on their cell phone about the incident too," one of the rangers replied. They thanked Dad and hustled on.

Dad watched the rangers climb the trail. *I'm relieved the park is responding to the emergency*, he thought to himself.

Dad sloshed on, exhausted from the lengthy ordeal and the lack of sleep. The path was difficult, so Dad had to take his time and watch his footing. He limped along in the relative safety of the forest, using his walking stick to balance and guide his steps. Finally, while plunging down a long, rocky, muddy section of trail, Dad sensed he was getting close to the car.

All of a sudden, Dad saw a building ahead. He recognized it as the trailhead bathroom. Dad trudged inside and went right up to the sink. He splashed his weary face with water and looked into the mirror. "Boy," he said to himself, "you look like you've been through the wringer."

Dad tried to pat down his matted hair but gave up a moment later, exiting the bathroom to go to the car. He got inside and shed all his wet clothes. Dad threw the muddy pile of gear into the back, put on a warm, dry shirt and pants, and glanced around the parking lot.

A few other hikers had also reached the safety of their cars and were packing up. Dad noticed several ranger cars and an ambulance parked nearby. A crew of rangers and paramedics were gathered outside one of the trucks.

Dad gingerly got out of the car to ask for more information. But his foot just couldn't take any weight on it, and his back was sore.

He stood outside for a moment more, then slid back into the car. *They have all the help they need, and I can always find out what happened later*, he told himself.

Dad took two aspirin and started the engine. "Maybe I shouldn't have tried this hike," he said. "But then again, this whole ordeal could have turned out a heck of a lot worse."

Dad backed out of the parking lot and began driving toward Estes Park and the Glacier Basin area.

• • •

The two rangers were talking about the emergency rescue on the Longs Peak Trail.

Mom heard this and quickly stepped closer. "Can you tell us what happened?" she asked urgently.

"I only know that someone was probably struck by lightning. They tried to get a helicopter up there, but the storm made it too dangerous. A crew is bringing the person down by trail."

Mom swallowed anxiously. "Do you know who it is?"

"That I don't," the ranger replied. "But I can call park dispatch to get any updated information for you."

• • •

As Dad drove into the park and headed toward the campground, he drove past the visitor center. Dad slowed the car down. *Hmm*, he pondered. *Is it*

possible they're waiting in there because of the weather?

Dad turned around and drove into the parking lot.

• • •

Morgan, James, and Mom followed the ranger toward a phone. As they walked past the front desk, a man wearily dragged himself in.

Everyone stopped and looked at the weather-beaten figure.

"Dad!" Morgan and James called out, running to him.

Mom let out a relieved sigh and also ran to Dad.

After the brief reunion, the visitor center ranger said, "I assume you won't be needing me to phone dispatch anymore?"

"No, thanks," Mom replied.

The family escorted Dad back up to the viewing room. Dad plopped down into one of the chairs. Morgan, James, and Mom stood nearby.

"So, what happened up there?" Morgan finally asked.

Dad took a long, slow, deep breath. He got a little choked up. "Well," he started, then stopped. Dad gulped.

"It's okay," Mom said, putting her arm on Dad's shoulder.

Finally Dad managed to speak. "I should have stayed behind with all of you."

Then Dad told the rest of his story. He described the hike at night, how cold it was, seeing the stars, the ghostlike forest, the sunrise, and climbing the boulder field. Dad finally got through all the details he could think of. He also described how high he went, the couple he met, and what had happened with his ankle.

Next Dad detailed how he barricaded himself against the weather and how he finally got down the mountain as fast as he could, despite the conditions.

He said he felt cold and numb the whole way down. "It was almost like being stuck in a bad dream," he told them. "I was so relieved to make it back into the forest."

He paused for a moment and stared out the window.

Morgan watched Dad. "What about the rescue?"

Dad continued with the rest of his story. "It was really hard to tell what took place up there," he admitted. "Everything was happening so fast, and…"

Dad stopped, looked outside again, and continued. "Either the person I saw was hit, or they just took cover like me. But I did see rescuers running up the trail, and in the parking lot."

Dad finally took a deep breath, finished with his tale.

"We're so relieved you are safe," Mom said.

"Thanks," Dad replied. "And what about all of you?"

Morgan, James, and Mom each related details about their adventure on the Fern Lake Trail.

"It really wasn't that bad for us," James concluded.

"Watching the storm from the backcountry cabin was kind of cool," Morgan admitted.

"I think the hardest part," Mom mused, "was not knowing if you were the one being rescued."

Dad looked at Mom, puzzled.

"We heard about the incident from the ranger at Fern Lake," Mom explained.

"Wow," Dad said. "The backcountry rangers are really kept informed here. That's good." Dad stood up and limped around the viewing room. "Well, while we're here, let's finally get a good look around, okay?"

James smiled and shook his head. "We can't. It's almost 5 PM."

And the Parkers all laughed.

Just before 8 AM, Morgan got up and took Dad's thermometer outside the tent. She placed it on the picnic table and waited for it to settle.

A few minutes later, Morgan crept back into the family's cocoon. Dad rolled over in his sleeping bag. "How is it out there?"

Morgan gave her family the morning weather report. "Well, it looks like a nice day. Right now the temperature is 37 degrees, but there's no frost. The skies are mostly clear, and the sun is lighting up parts of the campground."

James smiled. "Maybe it's your turn to start doing weather reports on TV."

"Maybe," Dad said sleepily, turning over. "I have a request. Can I stay in the tent just a little longer?"

So he did. Once it was past 9 AM, sunlight poured onto the tent, warming it quickly. Dad yawned and sat up. "I actually feel pretty rested!" he said out loud, surprised.

He slid outside to help make breakfast.

Mom smiled at her family. "Good morning, everyone, and welcome to another beautiful morning in the Rockies!" she announced.

Dad hobbled over to the car for more ingredients. James noticed Dad limp as he walked. "Let me help you," James said.

"My foot's definitely sore," Dad admitted as he and James carried food back to the table. "I'll have the doctor look at it when we get home."

When breakfast was ready, the Parkers sat and ate at the picnic table. By the time they cleaned up and packed everything, it was after 10 AM.

For a final time, the family drove over to the Park & Ride area, packing up for one last hike in the park.

Once more the Parkers took the bus up. They exited with a slew of others at Bear Lake.

The skies were partly cloudy by then, and the intermittent morning sun made it perfect weather for hiking. The family walked over to a bench, and James pulled out his park map.

"So," James said, reviewing the Bear Lake area trail brochure, "it's less than two miles to Emerald Lake. Not far at all."

They filled up their water bottles at the drinking fountain while Dad sat nearby and rubbed his foot. "You know," Dad began, "I think my ankle needs a day off. I'm going to pass on this hike."

Morgan, James, and Mom looked at Dad with surprise. "Are you sure?" Morgan asked. "We'll go slow."

"That's okay," Dad replied. "I'll just be holding you up. Besides," he added, "I'd like to look around Bear Lake."

Dad checked his watch. "It's almost 11 AM. How about we meet back here at this bench at, say, 1:30?"

"That should give us plenty of time," Mom agreed.

And with that, the Parkers again split up.

• • •

Dad pulled out his walking stick. He got up and used it on his tramp over to Bear Lake, just a short distance away.

A trail circled the lake. Many people were strolling along the mostly flat pathway. Dad joined them, stopping to read his nature guide at the paw print markers along the way.

At one stop, the pamphlet gave information about the park's geology. Dad read the guide, then inspected the rocks nearby. "Two billion years of mountain building," he said aloud, amazed.

Dad continued walking slowly along the path and eventually found a bench to sit on. He plopped himself down and noticed beyond the lake a familiar mountain looming above all others. *Ah, my old friend and nemesis, Longs Peak!* Dad exclaimed to himself, staring at the massive mountain. "One day," he said to the mountain, "I'll be back."

Then Dad rubbed his foot. "As soon as I get better," he added.

TAKING THE LONG VIEW

Longs Peak can be seen from over 100 miles away on the Great Plains. Native Americans used it to help navigate during their travels. The Stephen Long party of explorers visited the area in 1820, and, although Long didn't climb it, the mountain is named after him. Scaling Longs Peak is very challenging. Most people choose the Keyhole route, but because of weather, the time involved, and altitude issues, over half of the people who try don't make it to the summit.

Pretty Nymph Lake.

• • •

Morgan, James, and Mom trekked up the first part of the trail. This section was paved, and it was crowded with other hikers. Soon the family reached a small lake full of lily pads. "Nymph Lake," James announced while checking the trail map.

As they walked past the picturesque spot, Morgan pointed to the sky. "Look!"

Puffy cumulus clouds were dotting the sky.

"Hmm," Mom said.

And they hiked on.

• • •

At stop number twenty-two, Dad paused near a bunch of trees that were bent strangely. He read in his pamphlet that the weight of heavy snows had bowed the trunks outward, leaving "snow knees" behind. *Wow*, Dad thought. *There's so much to pay attention to in nature.* He hobbled on.

A couple of rangers walked past. Dad waved to them, and they said hello back. As they strolled along, Dad overheard one say to the other, "That was quite an ordeal on the mountain yesterday. But it could have been a lot worse."

Dad turned and called over, "I was up there. What happened?"

The rangers stopped and looked toward Dad. "Someone got struck by lightning up near the Keyhole. Were you near there during the storm?"

"I was below it. It was pretty bad there too. But I knew someone was in trouble. Is he okay?"

"She is mostly okay, now. Luckily she only has minor injuries and it wasn't a direct strike."

"Whoa," Dad said. "Thanks for letting me know."

The rangers continued on.

• • •

A short time later, Morgan, James, and Mom reached a second lake. This one was much different from the first. Dream Lake was situated in a deep mountain bowl. The narrow body of water was dotted with boulders.

"Wow!" Mom exclaimed while gazing at the scenery. "I can see why it is named Dream Lake."

"Dad would love it here," James said.

Morgan, James, and Mom spent a few minutes looking at the lake. "We'd better head on," Mom suggested.

• • •

Later, Dad stopped at another bench. He sat down and gazed out over the water and the spruce-fir forest surrounding it. Dad took a deep breath and admired the scenery. Then he read more from his nature guide. *I'm at 9,475 feet,* he realized. *This little lake is so high up!*

Dad stared into the clear water. He noticed several fish swimming near the shore. "Trout!" Dad said aloud.

Dad leaned over and watched the stout fish. *They sure are beautiful,* he thought to himself.

After a while, Dad got up and walked farther along.

• • •

Finally, Morgan, James, and Mom reached the end of the trail. The dark green–colored Emerald Lake was flush against high mountains. A couple of waterfalls splashed into it.

The three Parkers sat on some rocks near the shore. James checked his map. "I think we looked down on this lake from the Flattop Mountain Trail," he realized.

"I remember that!" Morgan said. "I think it's the best of the three lakes on this hike," she added.

"Dream Lake was cool too," James said.

"They each have their own personality," Mom concluded.

Morgan, James, and Mom spent several minutes at the lake, then walked back down the trail.

• • •

Dad paused in a cool, shady area and checked his watch: *12:30. I wonder how my family is doing.* He got up and slowly trudged along, taking his time while heading for the family's agreed-upon meeting place, a sun-sheltered area near the trailhead. He eventually returned to the trailhead. Some visitors were walking back to their cars. Others were waiting for the bus. Dad sat in a sun-sheltered area and watched the hikers come and go.

• • •

After Morgan, James, and Mom passed Dream Lake, they spent another moment or two soaking in the scenery there. Then they continued on, hustling past Nymph Lake on their final stretch to the trailhead. "We're getting close," Mom called out to her kids once they reached the pavement.

• • •

Dad decided to use his walking stick to hobble on the paved trail toward Nymph Lake. He was just a short way along when he saw his family coming down.

Dad stopped and let them come up to him, then they walked back together.

A few minutes later they arrived at the Bear Lake area.

"Let's go check out the lake," Dad spontaneously suggested. "I can't believe with all the hiking we've done, we haven't hung around there."

The family walked up to the nature path and sat on a bench. James and Morgan pulled out their journals.

This is James Parker reporting from Rocky Mountain National Park.

While we're here at Bear Lake I'm going to sketch some clouds in my journal so I remember what they look like, what weather they bring, and their names: cirrus, stratus, cumulus, and cumulonimbus.

It's the cumulonimbus clouds that keep bringing the thunderstorms wherever we are, it seems. I wonder if it's just Murphy's Law, as Mom says, or if it's always like this during summers in the Rockies.

Anyway, despite the crazy weather, Rocky Mountain is a beautiful place. Here are my favorite sites:

1. Emerald Lake

2. Mills Lake

3. Black Lake

4. Andrews Glacier Trail

5. Fern/Odessa Lake

6. Flattop Mountain

7. Trail Ridge Road

8. Old Lulu City

9. Elk near camp

10. Deer Mountain

Reporting from Rocky,

James Parker

Morgan wrote:

Dear Diary,

I really understand now how serious the weather warnings are for this area. If you decide to come to Rocky Mountain National Park, try to hike in the mornings, which are usually great. But on many summer days by afternoon or so, expect monster thunderstorms.

The weather and altitude of the park can be challenging, but it is absolutely worth coming. Rocky Mountain is a special place, even if you don't hike!

Here are my top ten sites:

1. Colorado River Trail
2. The tundra on Trail Ridge Road
3. The views from Deer Mountain
4. The Moraine Park Visitor Center
5. The elk on Trail Ridge Road
6. Glacier Gorge Trail
7. Andrews Glacier
8. Longs Peak, almost (I put that in for Dad)
9. Birding in the Beaver Meadows area
10. Flattop Mountain

Adios from Rocky Mountain National Park,

Morgan

The family caught the next bus down to the parking area. They drove out of the park, through Estes Park, and toward Denver.

On the way, a weather report came on the radio. "A chance of afternoon thundershowers again today in the mountains," the broadcast began. Dad turned off the station. "We know where that's going," he said, smiling.

The family got a hotel room in Denver. They would leave in the morning for the Denver airport and their flight home.

Later, the Parkers drove to Coors Field for a baseball game between the home team, the Colorado Rockies, and the Parkers' favorite team, the Los Angeles Dodgers.

In the fifth inning, the family was sitting in the bleachers eating hot dogs and popcorn. The Colorado cleanup hitter was at the plate.

It was a two ball, two strike count when the powerful slugger connected on a swing. He sent a towering fly ball way up into the bleachers, high over the Parkers' heads, for a home run.

The crowd went crazy.

"I hope that ball doesn't have altitude issues," James mentioned.

"Yeah, it was hit at least a mile above tree line," Morgan added.

"It probably ended somewhere up on Longs Peak," Dad concluded, and then the family all laughed.